Contents

GARY FORTY

Bible Storybook for kids

DANIEL:

Early Life Of Daniel In Babylon

The Captivity of Judah

T n the third year of the reign of Jehoiakim king of Judah came Nebuchadnezzar king of Babylon unto Jerusalem, and besieged it. And the Lord gave Jehoiakim king of Judah into his hand, with part of the vessels of the house of God: which he carried into the land of Shinar to the house of his god; and he brought the vessels into the treasure house of his god.

The opening verses of Daniel succinctly give the historical setting which includes the first siege and capture of Jerusalem by the Babylonians. According to Daniel, this occurred "in the third year of the reign of Jehoiakim king of Judah," or approximately 605 b.c. Parallel accounts are found in 2 Kings 24:1-2 and 2 Chronicles 36:5-7. The capture of Jerusalem and the first deportation of the Jews from Jerusalem to Babylon, including Daniel and his companions, were the fulfillment of many warnings from the prophets of Israel's coming disaster because of the nation's sins against God. Israel had forsaken the law and ignored God's covenant (Is 24:1-6). They had ignored the Sabbath day and the sabbatic year (Jer 34:12-22). The seventy years of the captivity were, in effect, God claiming the Sabbath, which Israel had violated, in order to give the land rest.

Israel had also gone into idolatry (1 Ki 11:5; 12:28; 16:31; 18:19; 2 Ki 21:3-5; 2 Ch 28:2-3), and they had been solemnly warned of God's coming judgment upon them because of their idolatry (Jer 7:24— 8:3; 44:20-23). Because of their sin, the people of Israel, who had given themselves to idolatry, were carried off captive to Babylon, a center of idolatry and one of the most wicked cities in the ancient world. It is significant that after the Babylonian captivity, idolatry never again became a major temptation to Israel.

According to Daniel 1:1, the crucial siege and capture of Jerusalem by Nebuchadnezzar king of Babylon came "in the third year of the reign of Jehoiakim king of Judah." Critics have lost no time pointing out an apparent conflict between this and the statement of Jeremiah that the first year of Nebuchadnezzar king of Babylon was in the fourth year of Jehoiakim (Jer 25:1). Montgomery, for instance, rejects the historicity of this datum.36 This supposed chronological error is used as the first in a series of alleged proofs that Daniel is a spurious book written by one actually unfamiliar with the events of the captivity. There are, however, several good and satisfying explanations.

The simplest and most obvious explanation is that Daniel is here using Babylonian reckoning. It was customary for the Babylonians to consider the first year of a king's reign as the year of accession and to call the next year the first year. Keil and others brush this aside as having no precedent in

Scripture.37 Keil is, however, quite out of date with contemporary scholarship on this point. Jack Finegan, for instance, has demonstrated that the phrase the first year of Nebuchadnezzar in Jeremiah actually means "the accession year of Nebuchadnezzar"38 of the Babylonian reckoning. Tadmor was among the first to support this solution, and the point may now be considered as well established.39

Jewish Youths Selected for Training

1:3-7 And the king spake unto Ashpenaz the master of his eunuchs, that he should bring certain of the children of Israel, and of the king's seed, and of the princes; Children in whom was no blemish, but well favoured, and skilful, in all wisdom, and cunning in knowledge, and understanding science, and such as had ability in them to stand in the king's palace, and whom they might teach the learning and the tongue of the Chaldeans. And the king appointed them a daily provision of the king's meat, and of the wine which he drank: so nourishing them three years, that at the end thereof they might stand before the king. Now among these were of the children of Judah, Daniel, Hananiah, Mishael, and Azariah: Unto whom the prince of the eunuchs gave names: for he gave unto Daniel the name of Belteshazzar; and to Hananiah, of Shadrach; and to Mishael, of Meshach; and to Azariah, of Abed-nego.

GARY FORTY

In explanation of how Daniel and his companions found the way to Babylon, Daniel records that the king "spake unto Ashpenaz," better translated "told" or "commanded," to bring some of the children of Israel to Babylon for training to be servants of the king.

Those selected for royal service are described as being "the children of Israel, and of the king's seed, and of the princes." The reference to the children of Israel does not mean that they were selected out of the Northern Kingdom which already had been carried off into captivity, but rather that the children selected were indeed Israelites, that is, descendants of Jacob. The stipulation, however, was that they should be of the king's seed, literally "of the seed of the kingdom," that is, of the royal family or of "the princes"—the nobility of Israel.

In selecting these youths for education in the king's court in Babylon, Nebuchadnezzar was accomplishing several objectives. Those carried away captive could well serve as hostages to help keep the royal family of the kingdom of Judah in line. Their presence in the king's court also would be a pleasant reminder to the Babylonian king of his conquest and success in battle. Further, their careful training and preparation to be his servants might serve Nebuchadnezzar well in later administration of Jewish affairs.

Daniel's Purpose Not to Defile Himself

1:8-10 But Daniel purposed in his heart that he would not defile himself with the portion of the king's meat, nor with the wine which he drank: therefore he requested of the prince of the eunuchs that he might not defile himself. Now God had brought Daniel into favour and tender love with the prince of the eunuchs. And the prince of the eunuchs said unto Daniel, I fear my lord the king, who hath appointed your meat and your drink: for why should he see your faces worse liking than the children which are of your sort? then shall ye make me endanger my head to the king.

Daniel and his companions were confronted with the problem of compromise in the matter of eating food provided by the king. No doubt, the provision for them of the king's food was intended to be generous and indicated the favor of the king. Daniel, however, "purposed in his heart" or literally, "laid upon his heart" not to defile himself (cf. Is 42:25; 47:7; 57:1, 11; Mal 2:2). The problem was twofold. First, the food provided did not meet the requirements of the Mosaic law in that it was not prepared according to regulations and may have included meat from forbidden animals. Second, there was no complete prohibition in the matter of drinking wine in the Law; but here the problem was that the wine, as well as the meat, had been dedicated to idols as was customary in Babylon. To partake thereof would be to recognize the idols as deities. A close parallel to Daniel's purpose not to defile himself is found in the book of Tobit (1:10-11, RSV) which refers to the exiles of the northern tribes: "When I was carried away captive to Nineveh, all my brethren and my relatives ate the food of the Gentiles: but I kept myself from eating it, because I remembered God with all my heart." A similar reference is found in 1 Maccabees (1:62-63, RSV), "But many in Israel stood firm and were resolved in their hearts not to eat unclean food. They chose to die rather than to be defiled by food or to profane the holy covenant; and they did die."70

The problem of whether Daniel and his companions should eat the food provided by the king was a supreme test of their fidelity to the law and probably served the practical purpose of separating Daniel and his three companions from the other captives who apparently could compromise in this matter. His decision also demonstrates Daniel's understanding that God had brought Israel into captivity because of their failure to observe the law. Daniel's handling of this problem sets the spiritual tone for the entire book.

Daniel's Request for a Ten-Day Test

1:11-14 Then said Daniel to Melzar, whom the prince of the eunuchs had set over Daniel, Hananiah, Mishael, and Azariah, Prove thy servants, I beseech thee, ten days; and let them give us pulse to eat, and water to drink. Then let our countenances be looked upon before thee, and the countenance of the children that eat of the portion of the king's meat: and as thou seest, deal with thy servants. So he consented to them in this matter, and proved them ten days.

Daniel's next step was to appeal to the steward who had immediate charge of Daniel and his companions for a ten-day test.

Daniel's Request Granted

1:15-16 And at the end of ten days their countenances appeared fairer and fatter in flesh than all the children which did eat the portion of the king's meat. Thus Melzar took away the portion of their meat, and the wine that they should drink; and gave them pulse.

At the conclusion of the test, Daniel and his companions not only were better in appearance but also were fatter in flesh than those who had continued to eat the king's food. Although God's blessing was on them.

God's Blessing on Daniel and His Companions

1:17-21 As for these four children, God gave them knowledge and skill in all learning and wisdom: and Daniel had understanding in all visions and dreams. Now at the end of the days that the king had said he should bring them in, then the prince of the eunuchs brought them in before Nebuchadnezzar. And the king communed with them; and among them all was found none like Daniel, Hananiah, Mishael, and Azatriah: therefore stood they before the king. And in all matters bf wisdom and understanding, that the king enquired of them, he found them ten times better than all the magicians and astrologers that were in all his realm. And Daniel continued even unto the first year of king Cyrus.

Nebuchadnezzar dream

One night, King Nebuchadnezzar has a strange dream. The dream stirs him up so he can not sleep anymore. He calls his wizards and says, "Explain to me my dream!" They answer, "Tell us what you have dreamed, O king." But Nebuchadnezzar says, "No! You shall tell me what I have dreamed, or I will have you killed! "But they say again," Tell us your dream and we'll explain it to you. "He says," You want to fool me! Tell me what I've dreamed of! "But they say," No one can do that. What you want is impossible. "

Nebuchadnezzar becomes so angry that he orders to kill all the wise men in the country. They include Daniel, Shadrach, Meshach and Abednego. Daniel asks the King to give him some time. Then he and his friends pray to Jehovah and ask him for help. What will Jehovah do?

Jehovah shows Daniel in a vision what Nebuchadnezzar dreamed and what it means. The next day, Daniel goes to the King's servant and says, "Do not kill the men! I can explain the dream. "The servant brings Daniel to

Nebuchadnezzar. Daniel says to the King, "God has shown you the future in a dream. You saw a huge statue. Her head was gold, her arms and chest were silver, her belly and thighs made of copper, her legs made of iron and her feet made of iron and clay. Then a stone was carved out of a mountain, and it hit the feet of the statue. The statue was smashed to dust and then blown away by the wind. The stone became a great mountain that spread all over the earth. "

Then Daniel says, "That's the meaning: your kingdom is the head of gold. The silver represents a kingdom that comes afterwards. Then there will be one like copper, and it will reign over the whole earth. The next kingdom will be as strong as iron. Finally, there will be a divided kingdom. Parts of it are as strong as iron and others weak as clay. The stone that becomes a mountain is God's kingdom. It will destroy all these kingdoms and stay forever. "

Nebuchadnezzar throws himself on the ground in front of Daniel and says, "Your God showed you this dream. There is no god like him! "Nebuchadnezzar does not want to kill Daniel anymore. He makes him the supreme of all wise men in the kingdom and ruler of the province of Babylon. Jehovah has really heard Daniel's prayer, right?

Nebuchadnezzar build a statue

Some time has passed since King Nebuchadnezzar's dream. Now he makes a huge statue of gold and sets it up in the plain Dura. All important men of the country should gather there. Shadrach, Meshach and Abednego are also to come. The King commands: "As soon as you hear the trumpets, harps and bagpipes, you must bow to the statue. He who does not bow will be thrown into an oven and burned. "Will the three Hebrews bow or will they remain faithful t Jehovah?

The King gives the order that the music should begin. Everyone bowed and worshiped the statue - only Shadrach, Meshach and Abednego not. Some men see this and say to the King, "These three Hebrews do not want to worship your statue." Nebuchadnezzar has the three summoned and says to them, "I'll give you another chance to worship the statue. If you refuse, I'll have you put in the oven. No God can save you from me. "They say," We do not need another chance. Our god can save us. But even if he does not save us, we will not worship the statue, O King. "

Nebuchadnezzar gets very angry. He says, "Heat the oven seven times more than usual!" Then he orders his soldier to "tie up these men and throw them in!" The oven is so hot that the soldiers die instantly when they come near. The three Hebrews fall into the fire. But when Nebuchadnezzar sees in the oven, he discovers not only three, but four men in the fire. Then he gets scared and he asks his officials: "Have not we thrown three men into the fire? But I see four, and one of them looks like an angel! "

Nebuchadnezzar approaches the stove and shouts, "Come out, you servants of the Most High God!" Everyone is amazed when Shadrach, Meshach, and Abednego come out of the fire. They are completely unhurt. Her skin, hair and clothes are not burnt at all. They do not even smell like fire!

Nebuchadnezzar says, "The god of Shadrach, Meshach and Abednego is really powerful. He sent his angel and saved her. There is no god like him. "

Do you always want to be as faithful to Jehovah as the three Hebrews - no matter what?

Nebuchadnezzar 2nd dream

One night, Nebuchadnezzar has a dream that terrifies him. He calls his wise men, but no one can explain the dream. Finally he tells Daniel the dream.

Nebuchadnezzar says, "In my dream, I saw a tree that reached to the sky. You could see him from all over the world. He had beautiful leaves and many fruits. In its shade, animals have rested and in its branches birds have built nests. Then an angel came out of heaven and shouted:> Turn the tree over and cut off its branches! But leave the tree stump with its roots in the ground. And put bands of iron and copper around the stump. His heart will be transformed from a human heart into an animal heart. Then seven times will pass. All men will know that God is the supreme ruler and that he can make the King whom he pleases. "

Jehovah lets Daniel know what the dream means. Daniel is startled and says, "O King, I wish the dream was about your enemies. But it's about you. The big tree that is blown away, that's you! You will lose your kingdom. And you will eat grass in the field like an animal. But you will become King again, because the angel has said that the tree stump should remain with its roots. "

One year later, Nebuchadnezzar walks across the flat roof of his palace and admires Babylon: "What a great city I built there! I am the greatest! "He has not finished yet, when a voice from heaven says," Nebuchadnezzar! You have just lost your kingdom. "

At this moment, Nebuchadnezzar loses his mind and becomes like an animal. He has to leave his palace and live with animals in the field. His hair becomes as long as eagle feathers and his nails become like bird claws.

Seven years pass. Then Nebuchadnezzar returns to normal and Jehovah makes him King of Babylon. Nebuchadnezzar says, "I glorify Jehovah, the

King of the heavens. Now I know that Jehovah is the supreme ruler. He humiliates proud people. And he can make a king who he wants. "

Belshazzar drinks from the vessel

Time passes and Belshazzar becomes king of Babylon. One evening he invites a thousand of the most important people in the country to a big party. He gets the golden cups that Nebuchadnezzar stole from Jehovah's temple. Belshazzar and his guests drink from the cups and praise their gods. Suddenly a hand appears and writes mysterious words on the wall of the banq uet hall.

Belshazzar is very shocking. He calls his wizards and promises, "Whoever explains these words to me makes them the third most powerful man in Babylon." The wizards try, but no one can explain the words. Then the q ueen comes in and says, "There's this Daniel. He used to explain dreams and puzzles to Nebuchadnezzar. He can tell you what the words mean. "

When Daniel comes, Belshazzar says, "If you can read and explain these words, I will give you a gold necklace and I will make you the third most powerful man in Babylon." Daniel replies, "I do not want your gifts. But I tell you what the words mean. Your father Nebuchadnezzar was proud and Jehovah humiliated him. You know what happened to him. But still you have no respect for Jehovah, but drink wine from the golden cups from his temple. That is why God has written these words: Mene, mene, tekel and parsin. They mean that the Medes and Persians will conquer Babylon and that you will no longer be a king. "

The soldiers of King Cyrus walk through the river and climb up to the gates of Babylon

The city of Babylon is protected by a deep river and thick walls. She seems invincible. But the same night the Medes and Persians attack . Cyrus, king of the Persians, diverts the river. So his soldiers can go directly to the gates of the city. When they arrive there, the gates are open! The soldiers storm into it, conquer the city and kill the king. Then Cyrus becomes the ruler of Babylon.

Right in the first year, Cyrus announces, "Jehovah has commissioned me to rebuild the temple in Jerusalem. Any one of his people who wants to help, may go. "70 years after the destruction of Jerusalem, many Jews are on their way home - just as Jehovah has promised. Cyrus also returns the silver and gold mugs and utensils that Nebuchadnezzar has removed from the temple. Did you notice how Jehovah needed King Cyrus to help his people?

Daniel in the lion's den

Another king of Babylon is the Median Darius. He notices that Daniel is a special man. That's why he sets him above the most important men in the country. The men are jealous of Daniel and want to get rid of him. You know that Daniel prays to Jehovah three times a day. Therefore they say to Darius, "O king, there should be a law that one may only pray to you. Anyone who does not keep the law should be thrown into a lion's den. "Darius likes the idea and he signs the law.

As soon as Daniel hears about the new law, he goes home. He kneels in front of an open window and prays to Jehovah. The jealous men storm in and catch him praying. Immediately they run to Darius and say, "Daniel does not obey you. He prays to his god three times a day! "Darius likes Daniel a lot and does not want him to die. That's why he's thinking all day long about how to save him. But not even the king can change a law he has signed. Therefore, Darius must give the order to throw Daniel into the pit, which is full of hungry lions.

Darius can not sleep at night because he is very worried about Daniel. In the morning he immediately runs to the lions' den and shouts, "Daniel, did your God save you?"

Darius hears a voice. It is Daniel! He calls back: "Jehovah's angel has shut the mouth of the lions. You have not done anything to me! "Darius is very happy! He orders Daniel out of the pit. Daniel does not even have a scratch. Then Darius orders: "Throw the men who accused Daniel into the pit!" As soon as the men are inthe pit, they are eaten by the lions.

Darius sends an order to his people: "Everyone should fear the God of Daniel, for he saved Daniel from the lion."

The 4 Beasts of Daniel and Revelation

The lion.

"The first was like a lion, with wings of an eagle. I watched until his wings were pulled out. It was lifted from the earth, it was put on its feet like a man, and it was given a human heart. "(Then 7: 4)

The first animal was a lion with wings. This Lion runs parallel to the gold from the dream of Nebuchadnezzar. The lion used to be the symbol for Babel. If you go to museums now you will find lions as a symbol for Babel. The lion is the king of the wild animals, just as the eagle is the king of the birds. In Jeremiah, Babel is also symbolized with a lion. (Jer 4: 7), (Jer 50: 17,18).

Wings can have multiple meanings. It can mean protection, freedom but also speed. (Hab 1: 6.8)

"He rode on a cherub and flew, yes, He was swiftly floating on the wings of the wind." (Ps 18:11)

These wings symbolize speed. Freedom and protection are of course not possible. Because Babel not only removed the Israelis as slaves, but they were also persecuted. These wings symbolize the speed at which Babel grew from a small state into the most influential in the region. Within 21 years, they had large parts of the region under control and ended the service. Then their expansion of conquest was stopped here symbolized with the wings being torn.

the human heart refers to the leaders who came after the death of Nebuchadnezzar. Nebuchadnezzar was converted to the God of heaven. You can read that in chapter four. After his death, kings came who ignored the laws of God. The empire was put on its pedestal and lost its lion status and turned into a human. The empire had passed away from God. And 23 years after the death of Nebuchadnezzar, the empire fell.

The bear.

"And behold, another animal, the second, looked like a bear. It focused on one side. It had three ribs in its mouth, between its teeth. The following was said to the animal: Get up, eat lots of meat. "(Dan 7: 5)

The second animal runs parallel to the chest and arms of silver from chapter two, and is identified as Medo-Persia. This bear erected on one side, representing the power difference in the empire. The Persians were more powerful and influential than the Medes. In the end, they even managed to gain full power. It is therefore depicted in the image with two arms that then become breasts. So here we see the power difference between the two peoples.

The teeth represent an army (Jl 1: 6)

The rib symbolizes tribes or peoples. Eve was created from the man's rib (Gen 2: 21,22). And said Eva was called because she is the mother of all living. (Gen 3:20) Eat a lot of meat refers to tribes or nations. The meat also comes back in Genesis. God let Adam fall into a deep sleep, then he took a rib and filled the rest with meat.

The three ribs are the three wars that Medo-Persia has fought against the nations. Lydie, Babel and Egypt respectively. At the height of their power, they had conq uered six times as much land as their predecessor Babel. That is why this beast ate a lot of meat.

The leopard.

"Then I looked, and there was another animal, like a leopard. It had four bird wings on its back and the animal had four heads. And it was given dominion. "(Dan 7: 6)

This animal runs parallel to the bronze of the statue of Nebuchadnezzar. That animal symbolizes Greece. The wings again symbolize speed like the lion's wings. Medo-Persia was defeated by the Greeks led by Alexander the Great. Within three years the empire fell and the Greeks had conquered the Medo-Persian empire. When Alexander the Great began his campaigns in 334 BC, until his death in 323 BC, he had conquered large parts of the then world.

After Alexander the Great died, four generals came to power and the empire was divided into four divisions. Pictured here as the four heads. These generals were Kassander, Lysimachus, Ptolemy and Seleucus.

The fourth beast.

"Then I watched the night visions, and behold, the fourth animal was frightening, horrible, and exceptionally strong. It had large iron teeth. It ate and shattered, and the rest trampled it with its legs. It was different from all the animals that had been before. And it had ten horns "(Dan 7: 7)

GARY FORTY

This beast is so frightening that Daniel cannot even describe what kind of beast it actually is. This beast is terrible. While those other animals were still identifiable to Daniel, he can hardly comprehend this. Daniel asks for an explanation of that fourth beast.

"Then I wanted to know the true meaning of the fourth animal, which was different from all the others - exceptionally frightening, its teeth were made of iron, its claws were made of bronze, it ate, shattered and the rest trampled on its legs - and ten horns that were turned upside down, and of the others that rose and for which three had fallen off, namely, those who had eyes and a mouth full of glory and whose appearance was greater than that of his companions. "(Dan 7:19 , 20)

This animal is the Romans, who dominated the world with their legions. The teeth of iron are not only a direct reference to the iron from the statue of Nebuchadnezzar. But their armies were also clad in iron. They had iron chest armor, iron shoulder protectors, iron shields, and their swords were made of iron.

Even the bronze of the Greeks can be found in this vision. The claws of bronze. And that is also historically true. We also see that in Daniel 4. The band of iron and bronze that had to remain in the earth. That symbolized Greece and the Romans. The Romans showed characteristics with the

22

Greeks. They have adopted Greek philosophy, Culture and also the language. They had the same gods. And even the spiritual church was partly Greek and partly Roman. In the year 1054 there was even a split between the Roman Catholic church and the Greek Orthodox church. In the end time it will most likely be formed into a unit again.

If we look at our current society, we have taken over much from both the Romans and the Greeks. We have taken over our entire society, culture, architecture, and philosophy from the Romans and the Greeks.

It was the Romans who ruled the entire region at the time of Christ, and it was Pilate who eventually had Christ crucified. The ten horns of the beast again show a fragmentation of the empire, just like the leopard with the four heads. Only ten kings will arise from this empire.

A horn is symbolized with a king. (Dan 8:21)

"And the ten horns indicate that ten kings will rise from that kingdom, and another will rise after them. It will be different from those that were there before. He will humiliate three kings. "(Dan 7:24)

Here it is clearly confirmed: "And the ten horns indicate that ten kings will arise from that kingdom." Ten kings will arise from the Roman Empire. Those ten kings or ten horns run parallel to the ten toes of iron and clay from the dream of Nebuchadnezzar, What a divided kingdom represents. (Dan 2:41) These ten empires were the Visigoths, The Franks, Sueven, The Allemans, Anglo-Saxons, Lombards, The Burgundians, the Herulen, Vandals and the Ostrogoths.

The Vision of a Ram and a Goat

In the first part of the vision, Daniel sees a ram with two large horns, the second horn becoming larger than the first. Then the ram pushes west and north and south, and no opponent can stand before him. Later in this chapter we are told that the two horns on the ram are the kings of Media and Persia. As we already know, the Persians came to the fore after the Medes (the second horn became longer) and this united empire continued to conquer everything for them. And indeed, they would go north and conquer Lydia, west and conquer Babylon, and under Cambyses II Cyrus' son would go south and conquer Egypt.

But then a unicorn male goat came from the west, which was running so fast that its feet did not touch the ground. He fell headlong into the ram, broke his two horns, knocked him down and trampled him.

We are told later in this chapter that this goat was the kingdom of Greece and the big horn the first king. Alexander the Great, king of Macedonia and hegemony of the League of Corinth (the federation of most Greek city-states) would come about 200 years later and within 10 short years conquer Persia and all its countries, thereby acquiring more territory than the Persian empire in 200 years.

That the combat action in the vision took place on a river is interesting, because of the three major battles that Alexander fought and won against the Persians, two of them took place in river valleys and in both Alexander's army across the rivers to attack the Persians, who on the other side were merged. These were the battles of the Granicus River in 334 BC and the Battle of Issus in 333 BC.

And just when the horn was broken when the goat became strong, Alexander died of fever at the age of 33, at the height of his power and conquest. Then four notable kings and kingdoms emerged from Alexander's fragmented empire, the details of which were discussed in the previous chapter. We can see that, although the animal is different, the description of Greece is very similar to the leopard in Daniel's vision as recorded in chapter 7.

The vision then jumps to the End Time, for we are told that the rest of the vision does not apply to the last times of these kingdoms, but that it refers to the time of the end. And from one of those four kingdoms came a little horn, a ferocious king, destined to rule a great empire in the last days.

It is believed by many scholars of biblical prophecy that the small horn of this vision was Antiochus Epiphanes, the last king of any interest in the Seleucid empire, one of the four kingdoms. That he was in the last days of the empire might be applicable - although he would remain in a weakened state a hundred years or more after his death - and he did things under his rule that seemed to be part of the world to have fulfilled. prophetic events mentioned in this chapter. But the fact that the vision refers to the "time of the end," meaning the time shortly before the Second Coming of Jesus, makes it impossible for him to be the person discussed in the rest of this chapter. And later we will see that an important comment from Jesus about Daniel's predictions in chapter 11 clearly shows these events as happening after his time on earth, and thus long after Antiochus.

Two characters appear in this vision to help Daniel understand what all this means. One is the angel Gabriel, who looked like a man to Daniel. The other is someone who instructs Gabriel to tell Daniel what the vision means. The second person who apparently does not see Daniel, but rather hears his voice from the middle of the river. Gabriel is one of God's archangels, and every voice that tells him what to do must be high for him. So scholars of the Bible believe that this voice belongs to Jesus.

Between what Daniel has seen and what Gabriel tells him, we get a lot of information about the little horn, which is understood as no less a personality than the devil man of the end, the antichrist. This "horn" is both a human and a spiritual entity, for he cannot do what he does, but only a mortal being.

The horn grows from one of the four areas that today correspond to 1) Greece, 2) Turkey, 3) Lebanon, Syria, Israel, Iraq and Iran, and 4) Egypt. - Only those at the moment we do not know. In Chapter 7 we saw the corresponding horn coming out of what the Roman Empire was, and that included all the countries mentioned except Iran and Iraq.

He extends his control to the south, to the east, and to the Glorious Land. The glorious land would be a reference to Israel, the holy homeland of Daniel

This horn, or king as it is mentioned later in the chapter, becomes as high as the army of heaven and throws part of it on the earth and tramples it. Revelation gives something similar about Satan: "His tail drew a third of the stars of heaven and threw them on the earth" (Revelation 12: 4). Although this horn is the Antichrist and not Satan, over time the Antichrist is completely possessed by Satan.

We are later told that this man is a ferocious looking guy who is aware of some very sinister plans and plans. He has a lot of power, but it's not really his own. This is repeated in Revelation, where it says that "the dragon [Satan] gave him his power, his throne and great authority" (Revelation 13: 2).

But he flourishes in everything he does and he destroys the powerful and also the holy people. We already read in the last chapter that the Antichrist wages war against the saints and has the upper hand, and here that information is given again. Not only are the saints mentioned this time, but also the mighty, meaning mighty nations that are against him. In a later chapter we will investigate who these nations and powers can be that he overcomes and destroys, even in their prosperity.

GARY FORTY

GIDEON:

Who was Gideon in the Bible?

T he account of Gideon's life is recorded in Judges 6:11-8:32. The backdrop for Gideon's biography begins with the Israelites being ravaged by the Midianites as a consequence of their disobedience to God (Judges 6:1). For seven years they faced invasions from the Midianites, Amalekites, and Eastern foreigners who ruined their crops and destroyed their cattle. Although they had been unfaithful to God by worshipping the gods of the Amorites, they cried out to God for His help without realizing why this was happening to them (Judges 6:6). And so God sends them a prophet to remind them of how the one true God had provided for them in the past and yet how quickly they had forsaken Him (Judges 6:8-10).

God hears their cries and graciously intervenes by sending an angel to Gideon to call him into service (vss. 11-14). Gideon, whose name means "cutter" or "cutter of trees," belonged to an undistinguished family of the Abiezrites, but from the angel's greeting we can assume that Gideon had already proved to be a mighty warrior (Judges 6:12). Though Gideon was a willing servant of God, he needed assurance that it was, in fact, God calling him to this divine service (vs.17). In accomplishing the mission set before him by God, Gideon proves himself to be faithful, a mighty warrior, a strong leader of men (Judges 7:17), and a diplomat (Judges 8:1-3). As such, he is included in a fitting testimonial for the great men of faith in Hebrews 11:32-34. Gideon was the fifth judge and renowned as the greatest of Israel.

The highlights of Gideon's life include his victorious battle against Israel's enemies. However, we mustn't overlook his amazing faith, by which he carried out God's mission and which was first put to the test and confirmed when he destroyed the Baal idols his father and the community had been worshipping (Judges 6:25-27). Gideon's battle triumph is preceded by God's anointing (Judges 6:34). It was no small feat that Gideon managed to enlist his tribesmen, the Abiezerites, to go into battle with him. These were the men whose idols he had destroyed and who had renamed him "Jerub-baal" (Judges 6:32). Before entering battle, Gideon's troops number 32,000, but in obedience to God he reduces them by 22,000 (Judges 7:2-3). Again in obedience to God he decreases the remaining 10,000 by a further 9,700, leaving him with just 300 men (vss. 7-8). This was against an enemy that is described as "thick as locusts" with "camels as numerous as the grains of sand on the seashore" (Judges 7:12). With the battle finally won, the people suggest that Gideon rule over them as their king, but he declines their accolades and tells them the Lord will rule over them (Judges 8:22-23).

Gideon had proved his faithfulness to God, and his obedience had required him to take a stand against his own father and tribe. And, although he feared his own people (Judges 6:24), from the three req uests he made for the Lord's confirmation of His will, it is evident he feared God much more. In battle he took on far greater odds than were realistic to mere mortals. When the Israelites wanted to honor him as their king for triumphing over their enemies and restoring Israel's pride, Gideon, recognizing God as the real victor in the battle, declines their req uest and affords the rightful sovereignty to God. This was a great test of Gideon's faithfulness, when he could so easily have succumbed to pride by accepting the people's honor. So, it is with great surprise that we see Gideon go on to compromise his faith by req uesting they all contribute gold from the plunder of the battle so he could create an "ephod," a breastplate or mask used in cultic worship (Judges 8:24-26). And, as we see in verse 27, it became a snare to Gideon and his family.

From Gideon's example we can learn that no matter how great the odds against us may be, our faithful God is sovereign, and He will always see us through whatever battles we face in life, as long as we remain faithful to His calling and obedient to His commands. "Trust the Lord with all your heart and lean not on your own understanding; in all your ways acknowledge Him, and He will make your paths straight" (Proverbs 3:5-6). We can also see how God uses ordinary people to accomplish His plans, although with Gideon, the key factor was his willingness to obey God.

Sometimes, the most difficult people to witness our faith to are our families. And we can see after Gideon destroys the false gods his family had been worshipping that he receives an anointing from the Lord. It was because of this anointing that he was able to accomplish the mission that God had set before him. And it is with God's anointing on our lives that we can truly claim "I can do everything through Him who gives me strength" (Philippians 4:13). Gideon had gone from being a warrior in hiding, threshing wheat at the foot of a hill out of sight of the enemy, to vanquishing the same enemy in battle. However, he was careful to ensure that it was God's will he was obeying. As the Apostle Paul wrote, "Do not conform any longer to the pattern of this world, but be transformed by the renewing of your mind. Then you will be able to test and approve what God's will is — his good, pleasing and perfect will" (Romans 12:2).

However, unlike Gideon, who had proved his faithfulness to God and received God's answers to his requested signs as an encouragement, we must not expect God to do likewise for those who request signs from God because of their doubts or weak faith

FULL STORY

The story of Gideon starts out with God not being very happy with his people, the Israelites. If you remember the Israelites were the ones God saved from Pharaoh. The people Moses led across the Red Sea on dry ground.

Hundreds of years had passed since then but throughout all of God's miracles they had experienced, they still did evil in the eyes of the Lord.

There were consequences for these actions. That means that when they did something wrong God didn't bless them but gave them into the hands of the Midianites.

The Midianites weren't their friends. They took or ruined all their crops and animals. The Israelties had to hide from them in caves.

After Israel had nothing left they finally cried out to God for help. God heard their cry (like he always does) and had a plan.

The cool thing about all this is that God wasn't happy with the Israelites but He still listened to them and answered their prayer!

This is where Gideon comes into the story. He was threshing wheat in a hidden place so that the Midianites wouldn't see him and steal the wheat, when an angel of the Lord came and sat next to him.

The angel spoke to him and said, "The Lord is with you, mighty warrior."

"But sir," Gideon replied, "if the Lord is with us why is all this bad stuff happening? Where are all the miracles our fathers (the people that crossed the Red Sea) told us about?"

The Lord replied to Gideon, "Go with all your strength and save Israel from the Midianites. I am sending you to do it."

Then Gideon started all the excuses. "But Lord, how can I save Israel? My people are the weakest in Manasseh and I am the smallest and the youngest in my family."

I think God probably smiled here, but He said "I will be with you, and you will defeat all the Midianites together."

Then Gideon asked God for a sign. He wanted to be sure this was really God that he was talking to. Gideon didn't have a Bible to follow and didn't know how or if God went around talking to people, he wanted to be sure.

First he prepared an altar as an offering for God. This was the way they gave gifts and ask for forgiveness to God before Jesus died on the cross.

He set his offering (meat and unleavened bread) down on a rock and fire came from the rock completely consuming the meat and bread. And the angel of the Lord disappeared.

Then Gideon realized that it was the angel of the Lord.

That same night the Lord told Gideon to take down the altar his father had built for a pretend God (Baal) and to cut down an Asherah pole (this was made for another god people wanted to worship).

The Israelites had started believing in these fake gods and that's why God had been angry with them. He is the only real and true God and these people were praying and giving offerings to pieces of wood and statues that can't do or hear anything.

So Gideon took ten of his servants at night (because he was afraid of getting caught from the people in the town) and tore down the altars.

The people were mad when they realized Gideon had wrecked their altars but they decided that if Baal was really a god he could punish Gideon. Of course nothing ever happened to Gideon because Baal isn't real.

Gideon still wanted to make sure that God would save the Israelites so he asked for another sign. He placed a piece of wool from a sheep on the ground. If there was dew only on the fleece and all the ground around it is dry, then he would know that God would save them.

When Gideon checked the wool in the morning it was soaking wet and the ground was dry. Still Gideon asked for one more sign...

This time he asked that the fleece would be dry and the ground would be wet. Sure enough, the next morning it was just as Gideon asked.

So Gideon gathered up an army and started out for the Midianite camp. Gideon was probably feeling pretty good about things. He had lots of men to help him fight and God promised he would help them win.

God had something a little different in mind. He told Gideon he had too many men in his army. He knew that Israel would think they defeated the Midianites on their own without God's help.

So God said to Gideon, "Announce to the people, 'Anyone whose afraid may go home now'." Amazingly twenty-two thousand of the men left! That's a lot of people! More than half of the whole army went home. Only ten thousand stayed.

Gideon still felt alright. At least they had ten thousand men, right? Not for long. The Lord told Gideon he still had too many men.

When they went down to the water for a drink the Lord told him, "Separate the men that drink the water like a dog and the ones that get on their knees and drink from their cupped hands."

I'm thinking this took q uite a while with all those men but Gideon did it. It's surprising, but only three hundred men got on their knees and drank from their hands. All the rest looked silly drinking like dogs!

God told Gideon that he only wanted the three hundred men and the rest were supposed to go home. This way when they won, the Israelites would know that God was in control with only three hundred men left.

Gideon didn't know how God was going to help them win. There were so many Midianites against just three hundred of them so he worried and wasn't getting any sleep. So, God decided to help Gideon and make him feel better about things.

During the night the Lord spoke to Gideon, "If you are still afraid that I'm going to help you win, go down in the valley with your servant Purah where the Midianites are staying and listen to what they're saying. You'll feel much better after that."

Guess what Gideon did? He was still afraid and took Purah and snuck down to the Midinaite camp. Just as he arrived he heard one of them talking to his friend about a dream he had. He was saying, "I dreamt that a round loaf of bread came rolling into our camp. It came so fast that it ran right into one of our tents and made it fall over."

His friend responded, "This must mean the sword of Gideon and that God will help him defeat the Midianites."

As soon as Gideon heard this he worshiped God and ran back to the camp. He returned and called out, "Get up, the Lord has given us the Midianite camp!"

Children's version bible stories: GideonHe divided all the men in three groups and gave them all trumpets and empty jars with torches inside.

Gideon and the men surrounded the camp in the three groups (remember they were up high looking down into the valley). When Gideon started to blow his trumpet the rest followed.

They blew their trumpets and yelled, "For the Lord and for Gideon!" Then they broke the jars they were carrying, holding onto the torches with one hand and the trumpet in the other hand shouting, "A sword for the Lord and for Gideon!"

When the Midianites heard this they started yelling and running around. Then when all the trumpets started again the Lord caused the Midianites to start freaking out and they stared to turn on each other with their swords.

The rest that got away were captured by the men of Ephraim by the Jordan because Gideon sent messengers ahead of them to let them know they were coming.

That was the day God saved Gideon and defeated the Midianites. Without God none of this was possible. I hope that after this Gideon learned his lesson and stopped worrying. With God nothing is impossible!

Next time you're in a tough situation know that God can give you strength and he wants to help you. Just ask and He will!

Accomplishments of Gideon in the Bible

He served as a judge over his people. He destroyed an altar to the pagan god Baal, earning the name Jerub-Baal, meaning contender with Baal. Gideon united the Israelites against their common enemies and through God's power, defeated them.

Gideon's Strengths

Even though Gideon was slow to believe, once convinced of God's power, he was a loyal follower who obeyed the Lord's instructions. He was a natural leader of men.

Gideon's Weaknesses

In the beginning, Gideon's faith was weak and needed proof from God. He showed great doubt toward the Rescuer of Israel. Gideon made an ephod from Midianite gold, which became an idol to his people. He also took a foreigner for a concubine, fathering a son who turned evil.

Life Lessons

God can accomplish great things through us if we forget our weaknesses and follow his guidance. "Putting out a fleece," or testing God, is a sign of weak faith. Sin always has bad consequences.

Hometown

Ophrah, in the Valley of Jezreel.

References to Gideon in the Bible

Judges chapters 6-8; Hebrews 11:32.

Occupation

Farmer, judge, military commander.

Family Tree

Father - Joash

Sons - 70 unnamed sons, Abimelech.

Ruth

The story of Ruth

R uth was a very fine Moabite princess who became the great-grandmother of King David. She was dissatisfied with the worship of her own people, and when the opportunity arose, she gladly gave up the privileges of the kings in her country and accepted a life of poverty among the people she admired.

Here's how it came about:

It was in the days when the judges ruled Israel. The children of Israel had become careless in observance of the Torah and had reduced God's punishment to themselves. There was a great famine in the land of Israel.

In Judah there was a certain man named Elimelech. He was a wealthy merchant, unused to hunger and poverty, and so he believed he could escape misery by moving to another location. So he took his wife Naomi and her two sons and moved to Moab.

Ruth became friends with this Jewish family. She learned to admire her laws and customs. The dissatisfaction she had already felt about the meaningless idol worship of her own people now turned into a positive objection. And when one of the sons asked her to marry him, she was happy and proud to accept. She did not regret what she gave up: her luxurious life in the palace, her royal title, her prospect of prosperity and honor in the future. She saw only the selfishness and mercilessness of her own people and the difference of the Jews to whom she had now committed herself.

Elimelech and his two sons died, and Naomi was a poor widow who did not know what to do or where to go. She therefore told Ruth and her other daughter-in-law Orpa (also a Moabite):

"My daughters, I have to go and I have decided to return to my hometown in Beth-Lechem. Things can not be too good there and there is no reason why you should suffer as well. Take my advice and go back to your parents. Your husbands are dead, and if you stay in your own country, you may find other men who can marry you. I have lost my sons forever, but you are young; You can get other husbands. "

Orpah looked sad, kissed her mother-in-law, and said goodbye to her. Ruth clung to Naomi in tears and asked her to come with her. With these touching words she implored her and said:

"Ask me not to leave you and return from your succession; because where you go I will go; and where you live I want to live; your people shall be my people, and your Gd my Gd; where you die, I will die, and there I will be buried; That's what the Lord does to me and even more, if you and me only part

Ruth knew exactly what she was doing. Naomi had reminded her of the difficulties the Jews were facing at any given time, but Ruth was determined to follow her mother-in-law and hold on to the belief in her adoption, which had grown so dear to her.

The future should prove that Ruth would rightly be rewarded for her great determination; But Ruth did not regret it in her poverty.

GARY FORTY

It was harvest time as Ruth and Naomi came to the land of Judah. They were both worn out from their journey, and Ruth prevailed upon Naomi to rest, while she herself would go out into the fields of Beth-Lechem and see what she could find to sustain them from hunger.

Ruth entered a field where many men were busy cutting barley, others were binding it into sheaves, while others were piling them onto wagons and carting them away.

A little hesitatingly, but spurred on by her hunger and by the thought that she must get something for her dear mother-in-law, Ruth went into the field and sat down for a while to rest and to see what luck she might have here.

Suddenly she was startled to hear a voice saying to her, kindly and gently: "God be with you, stranger! Come along into the field. Do not be bashful. Gather some ears of corn, and satisfy your hunger!"

It was Boaz himself, the owner of the field, who thus addressed Ruth.

Ruth thanked him and plucked some ears of grain. She then was going to depart, when the same kind voice urged her to stay awhile and gather pe'ah.

"What is pe'ah?" asked Ruth.

"Our Torah tells us that when the owner of a field has his grain cut, he is not to cut the corners of the field, but to leave them for the poor, the needy and the stranger to come and reap for themselves," answered Boaz.

"How wonderful!" exclaimed Ruth. And so she stayed and cut the corn from a corner of the field, and was then again about to go away.

"You do not need to go yet," urged Boaz. "Why not stay and benefit from leket (gleanings)?"

"What does leket mean?" again asked Ruth.

"According to our law, if a reaper misses some grain with his scythe, or drops some, he is not allowed to go back to gather that grain, and this must be left for the poor and the stranger," explained Boaz patiently to Ruth. He was finding her more and more attractive, and thought he had never seen such a noble-looking lady.

Ruth said nothing, but saw no reason for refusing to take advantage of the laws of the Torah, which she herself had so gladly embraced.

When she gathered a whole basketful, she went up to Boaz, thanked him very sincerely for his kindness, and got ready to depart.

"There is no need for you to go yet," coaxed Boaz. "There is still shikchah (forgotten sheaves) which you can take."

"The Torah is indeed limitless in its care of the less fortunate ones," said Ruth. "Now please tell me, what is shikchah?"

"When the owner of a field is taking his load of grain to his granaries, it is possible that he may have forgotten some sheaves in the field. Well the Torah forbids him to go back and get them; he must leave these forgotten sheaves for the poor, the widow, the orphan and the stranger."

Ruth was so happy with her good fortune. She had gathered almost more than she could carry. She and Naomi were now well provided for some time. She again thanked Boaz, who made her promise to come again. In the meantime Boaz had made enq uiries about the attractive stranger who had captured his heart, and he discovered that she was the widowed daughter-in-law of Naomi.

Ruth was full of excitement as she hastened to her mother-in-law and related all that had happened to her in the fields of Boaz. Naomi was happy that Ruth had been so successful and had found favor in the eyes of Boaz, the wealthy landowner. And so, when Boaz asked her to marry him, Naomi urged her to do so.

Now Ruth was unexpectedly rewarded with wealth and happiness. She and Boaz were blessed with children who became famous in history. She lived long enough to see her great-grandson David, who became the L⁻rd's anointed and beloved king of all the Jewish people.

For Ruth and Boaz had a son named Obed, who became the father of Jesse. And David, as you know, was the youngest son of Jesse.

The Book of Ruth Summary

Ruth and Naomi in Moab

Now it came to pass in the days when the judges ruled, that there was a famine in the land. And a certain man of Bethlehem in Judah went to sojourn in the country of Moab, he and his wife, and his two sons. And the name of the man was Elimelech, and the name of his wife Naomi, and the names of his two sons, Machlon and Kilyon, Efratites from Bethlehem in Judah. And they came into the country of Moab, and remained there.

And Elimelech, Naomi's husband died; and she was left, and her two sons. And they took wives for themselves of the women of Moab; the name of the one was Orpah, and the name of the other Ruth; and they dwelled there about ten years. And Machlon and Kilyon died, both of them; so that the woman was bereft of her two sons and her husband.

GARY FORTY

Then she arose with her daughters in law, that she might return from the country of Moab; for she had heard in the country of Moab that God **had visited His people in giving them bread. So she went out of the place where she was, and her two daughters in law with her; and they took the road to return to the land of Judah.**

And Naomi said to her two daughters in law: "Go, return each of you to her mother's house; and may God deal loyally with you, as you have dealt with the dead, and with me. May God grant you that you may find rest, each of you in the house of her husband." Then she kissed them; and they lifted up their voice, and wept.

And they said to her: "No, we will return with you to your people." And Naomi said: "Turn back, my daughters; why will you go with me? Are there yet any more sons in my womb, that they may be your husbands? Turn back, my daughters, go your way; for I am too old to have a husband. Even if I should say I have hope, even if I should have a husband tonight and should bear sons; would you tarry for them till they were grown? Would you, for them, refrain from having husbands? No, my daughters; for it grieves me much for your sakes that the hand of God **is gone out against me."**

And they lifted up their voice, and wept again. And Orpah kissed her mother in law; but Ruth held fast to her.

52

And she said: "Behold, your sister in law has gone back to her people and to her gods; go back after your sister in law."

And Ruth said: "Entreat me not to leave you, or to return from following after you. Wherever you go, I will go; and where you lodge, I will lodge; your people shall be my people, and your God **my God. Where you die, I will die, and there will I be buried; God** do so to me, and more also, if aught but death part you and me."

When she saw that she was steadfastly minded to go with her, then she left off speaking to her.

So the two of them went on until they came to Bethlehem. And it came to pass, when they were come to Bethlehem, that all the city was astir at their arrival, and they said: Is this Naomi? And she said to them, "Call me not Naomi ('pleasantness'); call me Marah ('bitterness"), for the Almighty has dealt very bitterly with me. I went out full, and God has brought me back empty. Why then do you call me Naomi, seeing God has testified against me, and the Almighty has afflicted me?"

So Naomi returned, and Ruth the Moabite woman, her daughter in law, with her, who returned out of the country of Moab; and they came to Bethlehem at the beginning of the barley harvest.

Ruth Meets Boaz

Now Naomi had a kinsman of her husband's, a man of wealth, of the family of Elimelech; and his name was Boaz.

And Ruth the Moabite said to Naomi: "Let me now go to the field, and glean ears of corn after him in whose sight I shall find favor." And she said to her: "Go, my daughter." And she went, and came, and gleaned in the field after the reapers; and she happened to come to a part of the field belonging to Boaz, who was of the kindred of Elimelech.

And, behold, Boaz came from Bethlehem, and said to the reapers, "God be with you"; and they answered him, "God, bless you." Then Boaz said to his servant that was set over the reapers: "Whose maiden is this?" And the servant that was set over the reapers answered and said: "It is the Moabite girl who came back with Naomi out of the country of Moab, and she said, 'I pray you, let me glean and gather after the reapers among the sheaves'; so she came, and has continued from the morning until now, scarcely spending any time in the hut."

Then said Boaz to Ruth: "Hearest you not, my daughter? Go not to glean in another field, nor go away from here, but keep close here to my maidens. Let your eyes be on the field that they reap, and go after them; have I not charged the young men that they shall not touch you? And when you are thirsty, go to the vessels, and drink of that which the young men have drawn."

Then she fell on her face, and bowed herself to the ground, and said to him: "Why have I found favor in your eyes, that you should take notice of me, seeing I am a stranger?" And Boaz answered and said to her: "It has been fully related to me all that you have done for your mother in law since the death of your husband; and how you have left your father and your mother, and the land of your birth, and have come to a people whom you knew not before. May God **recompense your deed, and may a full reward be given you by the L-rd, the God of Israel, under whose wings** you have come to take refuge."

And she said: "Let me find favor in your sight, my lord; for you have comforted me, and you have spoken gently to your handmaid, though I am not even like one of your handmaidens."

And Boaz said to her at the mealtime: "Come here, and eat of the bread, and dip your morsel in the vinegar." And she sat beside the reapers: and he reached her parched corn, and she did eat, and was replete, and left. And when she was risen up to glean, Boaz commanded his young men, saying: "Let her even glean among the sheaves, and do not reproach her; and let fall also some of the handfuls on purpose for her, and leave them, that she may glean them, and do not rebuke her." So she gleaned in the field until evening, and beat out what she had gleaned: and it was about an efah of barley.

And she took it up and went into the city, and her mother in law saw what she had gleaned; and she brought it out, and gave to her what she had left over after she had eaten her fill. And her mother in law said to her: "Where have you gleaned today, and where have you worked? Blessed is he who took notice of you." And she related to her mother-in-law where she had worked, and said: "The man's name where I worked today is Boaz."

And Naomi said to her daughter in law: "Blessed is he of God, who has not left off his steadfast love to the living and to the dead." And Naomi said to her: "The man is near of kin to us, one of our nearest kinsmen."

And Ruth the Moabite said: "He said to me also: You shall keep close by my young men, until they have ended all my harvest." And Naomi said to Ruth her daughter in law: "It is good, my daughter, that you go out with his maidens, and that they meet you not in any other field." So she kept close to the maidens of Boaz to glean to the end of the barley harvest and of the wheat harvest; and dwelt with her mother in law.

A Nighttime Encounter

Then Naomi her mother in law said to her: "My daughter, shall I not seek a home for you, that it may be well with you? And now is not Boaz of our kindred, with whose maidens you went?

"Behold, he winnows barley tonight in the threshingfloor. Wash yourself therefore, and anoint yourself, and put your raiment upon you, and get you down to the threshingfloor; but do not make yourself known to the man, until he has finished eating and drinking. And it shall be, when he lies down, that you shall mark the place where he shall lie, and you shall go in, and uncover his feet, and lay you down; and he will tell you what you shall do." And she said to her: "All that you say to me I will do." And she went down to the threshingfloor, and did according to all that her mother in law bade her.

And when Boaz had eaten and drunk, and his heart was merry, he went to lie down at the end of the heap of corn; and she came softly, and uncovered his feet, and laid herself down. And it came to pass at midnight, that the man was startled, and turned over; and, behold, a woman lay at his feet.

And he said: "Who are you?" And she answered: "I am Ruth your handmaid; spread therefore your skirt over your handmaid, for you are a near kinsman.

And he said: "Blessed be you of God, **my daughter; for you have shown more loyalty in the latter** end than at the beginning, inasmuch as you did not follow the young men, whether poor or rich. And now, my daughter, fear not, I will do to you all that you req uire; for all the city of my people knows that you are a virtuous woman.

"Now it is true that I am your near kinsman; yet there is a kinsman nearer than I. Tarry this night, and it shall be in the morning, that if he will perform to you the part of a kinsman, good and well: let him do the kinsman's part; but if he will not do the part of a kinsman to you, then will I do the part of a kinsman to you, as God **lives. Lie down until the morning."**

And she lay at his feet until the morning; and she rose up before one could recognize another person. And he said: "Let it not be known that a woman came into the threshingfloor." Also he said "Bring the veil that you have upon you, and hold it." And when she held it, he measured six measures of barley, and laid it on her; and he went into the city.

And when she came to her mother in law, she said: "Who are you, my daughter?" And she told her all that the man had done for her. And she said: "These six measures of barley he gave me; for he said to me, Do not go empty to your mother in law." Then she said: "Sit still, my daughter, until you know how the matter will fall; for the man will not rest q uiet until he finishes the matter today."

Ruth and Boaz Start a Family

Then Boaz went up to the gate, and sat down there; and, behold, the kinsman of whom Boaz spoke came by.

And he said: "Ho there, such and such a one! Turn aside, sit down here." And he turned aside, and sat down. And he took ten men of the elders of the city, and said: Sit down here. And they sat down.

And he said to the kinsman: "Naomi, who is come back out of the country of Moab, is selling a parcel of land, which was our brother Elimelech's; and I thought to advise you of it, saying: 'Buy it in the presence of the inhabitants, and in the presence of the elders of my people.' If you will redeem it, redeem it; but if you will not redeem it, then tell me, that I may know; for there is none to redeem it besides you, and I am after you." And he said: "I will redeem it."

Then said Boaz: "On the day you acq uire the field from the hand of Naomi, you must acq uire also from Ruth the Moabite, the wife of the dead, to raise up the name of the dead upon his inheritance." And the kinsman said: "I cannot redeem it for myself, lest I harm my own inheritance. Take my right of redemption for yourself, for I cannot redeem it."

Now this was the custom in former time in Israel concerning redeeming and concerning exchanging: to confirm all manner of transactions, a man pulled off his shoe, and gave it to his neighbor, and this was the manner of attesting in Israel. Therefore the kinsman said to Boaz, "Buy it for yourself," and drew off his shoe.

And Boaz said to the elders, and to all the people: "You are witnesses this day, that I have bought all that was Elimelech's, and all that was Kilyon's and Machlon's, from the hand of Naomi.

"Moreover, Ruth the Moabite, the wife of Machlon, have I acq uired as my wife, to raise up the name of the dead upon his inheritance, that the name of the dead be not cut off from among his brethren, and from the gate of his place; you are witnesses this day."

And all the people that were in the gate, and the elders, said: "We are witnesses. May God **make the woman that is come into your house like Rachel and like Leah, which two did build the** house of Israel; and be prosperous in Efrata, and be famous in Bethlehem. And may your house be like the house of Peretz, whom Tamar bore to Judah, of the seed which God shall give you of this young woman."

So Boaz took Ruth, and she was his wife; and he went in to her, and God gave her conception, and she bore a son.

And the women said to Naomi: "Blessed is God, who has not left you this day without a redeemer, that his name may be famous in Israel. And he shall be to you a restorer of your life, and a nourisher of your old age; for your daughter in law, who loves you, who is better to you than seven sons, she has born him." And Naomi took the child, and laid it in her bosom, and became nurse to it.

And the women her neighbors gave it a name, saying: There is a son born to Naomi; and they called his name Oved—he is the father of Jesse the father of David.

Now these are the generations of Peretz: Peretz begot Hetzron. And Hetzron begot Ram, and Ram begot Amminadav. And Amminadav begot Nachshon, and Nachshon begot Salmah. And Salmon begot Boaz, and Boaz begot Oved. And Oved begot Jesse, and Jesse begot David.

DAVID

David the Shepherd

David's Ancestors

Davíd was born in Beth-Lehem, in the land of Judah, in the year 2854. He was only ten generations removed from Judah, one of Jacob's twelve sons.

David belonged to the princely family of his tribe, which had given Israel princes and leaders. One of David's early ancestors, Nachshon, the son of Aminadav, won fame at the crossing of the Red Sea, after the liberation of Israel from Egypt. He was the first to jump into the sea, whereupon the sea was divided for Israel. Since then, Nachshon was the most honored of all the princes of Israel. (He was the first to bring his offerings to the Mishkan, which was erected in the desert in the following year).

David's great grandfather, Boaz, or Ibzan, was the tenth Judge of Israel. He was one of the greatest scholars and most pious men of his generation. His estates were many, and his generosity was renowned.

When Boaz was eighty years old, he married Ruth.1 Ruth was a member of the Moabite royal family. Her grandfather was the powerful King Eglon of Moab. Yet Ruth preferred to become an ordinary Jewish woman, rather than a royal princess of Moab. All her trials and misfortunes did not dampen her great devotion to her newly acquired people. Even among the modest and fair maidens of Judah, Ruth stood out with a charm of her own; her modesty and piety, her selflessness and devotion became known far and wide. But how richly Ruth was rewarded! She became a princess in Israel—the wife of the ruling Judge, and the great-grandmother of King David. She lived long enough not only to see the glorious reign of King David, but also to see Solomon succeed to the throne of a great and glorious Land of Israel.

Throughout the years, the great traditions of the noble family, going back to Judah and Jacob, were maintained by the house of Jesse, David's father. Here was a house of scholarship, piety, kindness, generosity and wealth. And the noble traits of all his great and famous ancestors were bestowed upon David.

David Anointed

Soon God appeared to Samuel and told him to go to Beth-Lehem, where he would find the future king among one of the sons of Jesse. Samuel was to anoint the chosen one as king.

The prophet went to Beth-Lehem on the pretext of holding Divine services there, for he feared lest Saul detect his true purpose. Once in Beth-Lehem, Samuel imparted his secret to Jesse. Jesse presented to the prophet each of his seven sons in turn. David was absent, tending the sheep. Although they were all men of laudable q ualities, none of them qualified for this high position. "When Samuel was informed that Jesse's youngest son was in the field tending the flocks, he demanded that he be brought to him immediately. Seeing David, Samuel knew by Divine inspiration that he was the chosen one. Samuel then anointed him as the future king of Israel. From that day the spirit of G‐ d rested on David.

Saul Stricken With Melancholy

Almost simultaneously with the anointment of David, Saul was stricken with an evil spirit which threw him into a deep melancholy. The king's friends and courtiers noticed this sudden change and advised him to seek a good musician to ease his mind with the strains of sweet music. David, the future Psalmist, had already become known for his wonderful music as well as for his divine poetry. David was summoned to the king's court, where his sweet music on the harp helped to set the king's troubled mind at ease. Little did Saul know that the young lad who was playing before him was destined to be his successor.

SAUL, ISRAEL'S FIRST KING

There is no doubt that Samuel obeys God's commandments and is blessed for doing so, but things are different with his sons. They 'gain unjust profit, let themselves be bribed and bend the law'. The Israelites use this situation as an occasion to ask for a king to rule over them. They are also afraid of invasions by neighboring peoples. The request of the Israelites hits Samuel hard. But God assures him that by asking for a human king, they not only reject Samuel, but in reality they reject God as their king. Samuel warns them of the great burden it will take for them to have a king, but they still insist. They want to be like the surrounding nations. Jehovah shows his displeasure at her decision, by raising a storm that does not correspond to the season. But he does not turn his back on his people. He chooses a king: Saul, a modest man who towers all over his head and shoulder to his people and really has the look of a king. Samuel first anoint Saul secretly and then publicly, letting Saul proclaim king over the nation of Israel (1st Sam. 8: 1 to 10:27).

First, Saul proves to be a capable king. He unites the armed forces of Israel and defeats the Ammonites, who had threatened the men of Jabesh, whose city they besieged, a sadistic treatment. At this time, Samuel keeps his farewell speech, so to speak. He reminds his people how righteous and honest he has directed Israel all the days of his life, and repeatedly calls on him to fear and faithfully serve Jehovah.-1 Sam 11: 1-12: 25 .

After that, King Saul commits one mistake after another, failing to obey God's commandments. An emergency occurs when a great Philistine army threatens to attack. Saul is told to wait for Samuel to offer sacrifices and thereby implore Jehovah's help. Because Samuel is late and appears to be in dire straits, Saul improperly ignores the order to wait and delivers burnt offerings and community sacrifices. Immediately afterwards, Samuel appears. Jehovah rejects Saul as King for his presumptuous impatience: "Because you did not keep what Jehovah commanded you" (1 Sam 13: 1-23).

Once again, Saul makes a grave mistake by disobeying Jehovah's command to completely eradicate the Amalekites. Centuries before, the Amalekites had insulted Israel's stragglers, who were exhausted and exhausted on their journey through the wilderness (Deuteronomy 25: 17-19). Because Saul, along with the people, has spared the choicest of herds and Agag, king of the Amalekites, Samuel tells him, "Does Jehovah have as much pleasure in burnt offerings and sacrifices as in obeying the voice of Jehovah? Please refer! Obeying is better than sacrificing. , , Therefore, because you have rejected the word of Jehovah, he rejects you that you are not king. "After that, Samuel no longer sees Saul, though he mourns for him very much (1 Sam.15: 1-35).

David and Goliath

The Giant's Challenge

The Philistines had not been entirely subdued, and they again determined upon warfare. They entered the territory or Judah, and pitched their camp in a hilly country between Shochoh and Azekah. Saul entrenched himself with his men on an opposite height. A wide valley separated the two armies. Suddenly a man of abnormal height and strength emerged from the Philistine ranks. He was covered completely with the heaviest armor. Stepping midway between the two armies, he challenged the Jewish army to send forth a man who would dare to oppose him in single combat. The sight of this giant, armed to his teeth, struck terror into the hearts of the Jews. Day after day Goliath flung his challenge at the Jews without receiving an answer.

At that time David was at home caring for his father's sheep. His three older brothers were serving with Saul's army. Jesse called David and req uested him to take some provisions to his brothers. David arrived at the Jewish encampment just when Goliath was again defying Israel to produce an opponent to stand up against him. Surprised at the lack of courage of his brethren, David showed by his interest in the matter that he was willing to match his strength against that of the giant. He was immediately brought before Saul. At first Saul refused to send this youth against the veteran Goliath. Then David, anxious to obtain the king's consent, related his successful encounters with a lion and a bear and concluded, "The L-rd that delivered me out of the paw of the lion and out of the paw of the bear, He will deliver me out of the hand of this Philistine." Yielding at last, Saul said, "Go, and the L-rd be with thee."

David's Victory

David donned Saul's suit of armor, which the king offered him. But, when he saw how enviously the king eyed him, David pretended that the armor was too cumbersome for him, and he returned the suit to Saul. He took his staff in one hand and his sling in the other; and choosing five smooth stones out of the brook, he put them into his shepherd's bag, which he threw round his shoulder. Thus armed, he drew near to Goliath. The Philistine came forth, preceded by his armor-bearer; but when he saw the fair and ruddy youth he exclaimed disdainfully: "Am I a dog, that thou comest to me with sticks?" and he cursed him by his gods. "Come to me," he continued, "and I will give thy flesh to the fowls of the air and to the beasts of the field." But David, conscious of his good cause and inspired by it to a sublime courage, replied, "Thou comest to me with a sword and with a spear, and with a shield, but I come to thee in the name of the L-rd of hosts, the G-d of the armies of Israel, whom thou hast defied... And all this assembly shall know that the L-rd saves not with sword and spear; for the battle is the L-rd's, and He will give you into our hands." The Philistine, enraged by this bold reply, advanced towards the youth. Now David quickly drew a stone from his bag, and placing it in his sling, flung it at the forehead of the Philistine. It pierced the head of the giant, who fell upon his face to the ground. Running near and grasping the large sword of his fallen foe, the triumphant David cut off his head. Seeing their hero prostrate, the Philistines fled in panic, and the Jews pursued them as far as Ekron and Gath.

Why did God reject Saul because he made sacrifices?

Saul was not expressly rejected as a king for making sacrifices, but because he did not obey a direct command that God had given him through the prophet Samuel.

Samuel had told Saul, "Go down to Gilgal before me. I'm sure to come down to sacrifice burnt offerings and community sacrifices, but you have to wait seven days to come to me and tell you what to do. "But Saul, worried that all his army would leave him, offered that sacrifice just before Samuel arrived.

"You did something stupid," Samuel told him. "You have not kept the commandment that the Lord your God has given you. If you had, he would have built your kingdom over Israel for all time. But now your kingdom will not stand; The Lord has sought a man after his heart, and appointed him ruler of his people, because they have not kept the command of the Lord. "In other words, the punishment for this total disobedience to a direct command of God was that Saul would not do it, was the founder of a royal dynasty; While he would remain king, his descendants would not rule for him.

Second, however, this disobedience led to Saul gaining priesthood privilege.

Saul imitated the model of the Canaanite Priest-King instead of respecting the separation between the kingship and the priesthood, which was enshrined in the Law of Moses.

Saul later denied another direct command from God when he was again commanded by the prophet Samuel to destroy the Amalekites completely. Instead, Saul kept her King Agag alive as a war trophy, and his soldiers kept the best of the cattle "sacrificing" to the Lord as part of a great feast they would enjoy. Samuel again asked Saul, "Why did you disobey the Lord?" The punishment for total disobedience this time was that Saul would not even remain king for his natural life; he would die early and be followed by "one of his neighbors" - not one of his own offspring.

Saul's Cursed

Saul was Israel's first king. His unwise approach to leadership got him in trouble with the Lord over and over again. In this story, when the Israelites are battling the Philistines, Saul declares:

"Cursed is the man who eats food this day." And the people were faint. (1 Samuel 14:28)

This curse ends up affecting Jonathan, Saul's son, who wasn't present, having already gone on a daring raid.

This is just one of the many things Saul said and did that was just a bad decision. The story of Saul, Jonathan and David at times can seem a lot like a soap opera drama. The story basically has this plot: Saul does dumb things while David and Jonathan wait for David to become king. Inside this story line, there are deeper truths at play.

On a spiritual level Saul's approach represents how, if you don't have an understanding of the Word, you get off track. If you don't learn to think from the Word on issues in your life, you will get into trouble again and again. You are not going to be protected from all the falsity in the world and likely will suffer for it.

We need to learn how to think from the Word. This process is represented first by Saul's approach, then by Jonathan's approach, and then by David's approach.

Saul represents the letter – the literal meaning - of the Word. Sometimes he also represents obedience to that literal meaning. In simple terms, Saul represents the way we are when we don't want to think hard about how to live. It's like saying, "Just give me the rules and don't make me think about it." This approach can — and does - serve us for a time. As Israel's first king, Saul signifies a necessary step on the path of spiritual rebirth. But it's not very effective for long; it is too susceptible to falsities. Our progress can't last if we don't understand why we believe what we do.

David, who will be the second king of Israel, represents the spiritual sense of the Word - really understanding the Word, and understanding how God works. We can see this attitude in David's first Psalm:

"Blessed is the man who walks not in the counsel of the ungodly… but His delight is in the law of the Lord, and on His law He meditates day and night." (Psalms 1:1-2)

Jonathan is the son of Saul, because genuine truth is contained in the letter of the Word. He is David's best friend because genuine truth fully agrees with the spiritual sense.

If we don't come to have an understanding of the Lord's true character like David, we - like Saul - may inadvertently persecute the truth without knowing it. When we are not really searching the Word for answers we can be led this way and that. We may even find ourselves persecuting those who stand up for real truth because we have not looked at the Word ourselves to seek the truth. Today many who stand up for marriage being as God defined it in

Genesis being between and man and a woman, are persecuted because people are not searching the Word themselves. If we are not seeking the Word for its truth on marriage we can fall, like Saul, into persecuting the truth of the Lord's Word.

Throughout Saul's life he is at war with the Philistines, and can never seem to completely defeat them. His lack of deep understanding prevents it. In this story, Jonathan points this out:

"My father has troubled the land. Look now, how my countenance has brightened because I tasted a little of this honey. How much better if the people had eaten freely today of the spoil of their enemies which they found! For now would there not have been a much greater slaughter among the Philistines?".

DAVID AND SAUL

David is anointed king and comes to Saul at the royal court From 1 Samuel 15: 10-29 / 1 Sam. 16, 1-23

1. God shows Samuel the new king God was glad when he saw how David did his work faithfully and silently, singing his songs for him and talking to him. As much as God rejoiced over this shepherd, so little did he rejoice over another man in the land. From the outside, this man was beautiful, strong,

rich, powerful. He had many servants, many horses, chariots and soldiers; it was King Saul.

In the heart, however, Saul was not gorgeous, but filled with hatred and rage. He no longer wanted to obey God and, as king, decided everything himself. God decided, "Saul turned his back on me. He does not obey me anymore. Such a man harms my people. He can no longer govern it, otherwise he will lead the people away from me. "That is why God spoke in the night to the prophet Samuel. A prophet is a man who clearly hears God and passes on to others what God has said. God gave Samuel a clear order. A short time later, the Prophet stood before King Saul. The king greeted him cheerfully. But Samuel said with a straight face, "The Lord has talked to me last night. I have something to tell you. "" Just say, I'm listening! "Saul said. Samuel continued, "God has made you king over his people. He has given you clear orders to make the people well. Why did you not obey the Lord? You rebelled against God, so he deposed you as king. You will not rule much longer! "After Samuel said that, he turned around and started to go away, Saul was very scared and did not want to let him go, he grabbed Samuel's coat to hold him back, but the fabric ripped and the king Only held a small piece of cloth in his hand. Samuel said: "The same is the way the Lord has torn you of control of Israel today. Another will become king more worthy than you. "Then he turned away and left. He was very sad that God could no longer need Saul as king. He loved him. So God said to Samuel, "How long do you still want to be sad about Saul? In my eyes, he is no longer King of Israel.

Make your way to Bethlehem. Go there to Isai, for I chose one of his sons to be king. "Samuel was startled. "God, how can I do that? If Saul finds out, he'll kill me. "He knew Saul well and knew he wanted to remain king at all costs. Then God said, "Take a young cow and make a sacrificial feast. Invite Isai and his sons. Then I will show you exactly which son you shall anoint with the king. "Samuel was reassured there. If he made a sacrifice, it did not occur. And the ointment could be done in secret.

2. Samuel in Bethlehem So Samuel took out the big silver-studded horn and filled it with fragrant oil. Then he set off with a farmhand and a few animals. At that time, the ancient prophet was seldom seen on the journey. There was a great commotion among the people of Bethlehem when the venerable, grave man came in through their gate. Startled, the city's leaders approached him and asked, "Samuel, your visit does not mean anything bad?" "No, no," he reassured her. "I came to make a sacrifice. Get ready! Wash yourself and come to the party with me. And you too, Isai, come with your sons! "This sacrifice was a thank offering, so only a few pieces of the beast were burned for God on the altar. The rest was cooked and then sat together and ate each other this meat. Soon everything was ready. Samuel was full of expectation. Who will God choose? Who will be the new king? More and more families

came to the party. There also appeared Isai with his seven sons. Samuel

immediately noticed the eldest. His name was Eliab and he was a tall man,

handsome and strong. Now Eliab was standing in front of Saul. He almost

looked like Saul used to. That inspired the old prophet. "Ha, that will be the

new king!", He thought. "God takes the greatest and most beautiful!" And he

almost got up and anointed the young man. But at that moment he heard

God's soft voice inside: "No, that's not it. Do not be impressed by its

appearance and size! I look at something other than the humans. It's

important for people to see what they see with their eyes. I, on the other

hand, look every person in the heart. "Samuel was astonished, but then said

to Eliab," No, you are not. "Then he let the next son step forward. This was

Abinadab, a smart, handsome man. But again it sounded in Samuel's heart:

"No, that's not it." Now came the next: Samma. Samuel took pleasure in this

strong fellow, but God said again, "No, he is not." Then came the fourth, the

fifth, the sixth, the seventh son. And every time it said in Samuel's heart:

"No, it is not." Samuel felt very strange when all seven sons were over and

God had said no "yes". Did not he understand him correctly? God had said it

was one of the sons of Isai. So there had to be one more. So he asked, "Isai,

are they really all your sons?" Only then did the youngest come to mind to

the father. He had not thought to get him. What should be the smallest in

shepherd's clothes at such a festival? And he said, "Yes, we have one more,

the youngest. He protects the sheep. "Then Samuel said:" Then let him come immediately!

We will not be celebrating the festival without him. "That sounded odd to the brothers. Because of David, should they wait for the food? But one of them q uickly had to go and get David.

3. David is chosen David was out in the pastures with his sheep, when suddenly a brother ran by and shouted, "Come on, David, come! The prophet Samuel is here! He wants to see you. "David obeyed immediately, leaving the sheep to his brother and running home. He did not have much time, so he could not wear nice holiday dresses. He was only able to wash for a short time and soon after stood with reddened cheeks and sweat on his forehead in front of the men. Samuel got up and looked closely at the young shepherd. Then he smiled. David was a beautiful young man. He had an upright frame, was tanned and had clear, friendly eyes. Samuel heard in his heart, "That's him. Oint him! "The anointing meant that someone was chosen for something very special by God. Samuel liked to obey. He took the salbhorn and poured oil over David's head. He prayed for that. At that moment, something happened to David: The Spirit of God came into him and stayed in him from then on. He preferred God even more and wanted to make him even more enjoyable. God's Spirit gave him wise and wise words in his mouth and good thoughts in his mind; He made him happy and happy. Samuel saw that and was happy. Samuel understood it now: God saw things

that he had not found in any of his brothers with the young shepherd: love for God, obedience, a great trust in him and therefore courage. Now they celebrated together a happy party.

4. David comes to the royal court

David was anointed king, but he was not king for a long time yet. Saul lived and still governed. But God has everything under control and he set it up so that David soon came to the royal court. Because with King Saul a change had happened. Again and again he sat dully and gloomily on his throne, did not speak for days and just stared straight ahead. Then he shot up again, shouting and hollering so that people thought he was not quite right in his head. How did that happen? The Bible explains it simple and clear: Saul had disobeyed God, so God's spirit had gone from him and an evil spirit had come over the king. That's why fear and evil thoughts tormented him again and again. If he sat there so dead-sad, then he was sorry for his servants. And one day one of them said, "My king, you know that a bad spirit torments you. Let's look for a good harpist. Every time you have such cloudy thoughts the man will play and then you will feel better. You just have to order it, then we'll get one. "Saul looked up for a moment and said," Yes, look for one. "Another servant said," I know a young man I once saw. He is a son of Isai from Bethlehem. He can play the harp very well and he is brave. He finds the right word in every situation and he looks good. You realize that God is with

80

him. "Saul sent messengers and David was brought. So David came to the royal court. He could actually help Saul. When another bad fit came over Saul, David immediately took his harp and played. And again and again the music brought relief to Saul. He felt better and the evil thoughts left him alone. God had it that way. Saul calmed down and David learned a lot. If he was to become king, he could not claim the throne from the sheep

He had to know how a royal court was going to and fro. He could learn everything now.

JONATHAN LOVES DAVID

Jonathan loves David

So the young shepherd boy came to the royal court in Jerusalem. There he met Jonathan know. He was one of the sons of King Saul. Jonathan loved the charismatic David. The Bible says he loved David like his own life. And as a token of his love and loyalty, he gave David his armor, his sword, his bow, and his belt.

After David's conversation with Saul, Jonathan David joined in his heart, and Jonathan loved David like his own life, and he made a covenant with David because he loved him like his own heart, and took off the coat he wore and gave him David, as well as his armor, his sword, his bow, and his belt. " (1 Samuel, chapters 18: 1-4)

This biblical passage is remarkable. Jonathan gave himself entirely to David. He took a high risk. He made himself vulnerable, showed himself without visor and protection. At the time, that was very atypical behavior for men. What guarantee did Jonathan have that David would not take advantage of this? None. His love knew no bounds. He trusted David. And he even made a covenant with him. And David agreed to the covenant. However, it can not be seen from the biblical passage what David thought about the covenant.

It was a fateful moment. The king's son swore allegiance to the shepherd's son. What a reversal of the hierarchy! Was Jonathan not realizing he was massively reducing his chance of succession to the throne? Did not he care that, as a son of a king, he should actually strengthen his influence and power instead of promising his loyalty to a man of a simple shepherd family? Could that work out?

In fact, questions of status, power and influence stood between them. But Jonathan did not care. He made David a warrior and taught him all about warfare. And David became a successful warrior. He won battle after battle against the Philistines and became widely known beyond the king's court.

King Saul watched this development with suspicion. He did not like that David and Jonathan were enjoying themselves. He was also jealous and jealous of David. David seemed to succeed in everything he tackled. He had slain the strong Goliath with his wisdom. And in other battles David always emerged victoriously. Saul, on the other hand, became more and more melancholy and immovable. He saw his power as king in danger. David had done a lot for him. But he had become too powerful and popular. Saul only saw him as a dangerous competitor for power and honor. He had to stop David's influence. So he decided to kill David. David had known that and had not returned to the court of King Saul after a battle.

Saul's development was tragic. He realized that what happened to David as a young man was what happened to David. He had been chosen, anointed, and made a king. He had been popular, powerful and strong. And now this Shepherd Son from Bethlehem came along and stole the show for him. He was furious with anger.

It must have been a terrible situation for his son Jonathan. He experienced the anger and despair of his father. And at the same time he had fallen for David. He was wiped out between the two. And he seemed to forget about his own destiny as a potential successor to Saul. Or she was not important to him. Instead, Jonathan campaigned for David with his father. He mediated and spoke out for David. At first he succeeded, and David returned to the royal court.

But the apparent peace did not last long. Saul fell into melancholy again. David played for him on a lute to cheer him up. He had done so often at the beginning of his time at the court for the king. But instead of being grateful, Saul threw a spear at him. As a result, David finally fled the royal court. He made a secret meeting with Jonathan. Now David took command. He asked Jonathan to give his father an excuse for why David would not attend a feast at the court. But Saul recognized the excuse and became even angrier. Full of rage, he yelled at his son Jonathan:

"Son of a dishonorable mother, I know very well that you have chosen the son of Jesse, to you and your mother, who bore you, to shame! But as long as the son of Jesse lives on earth, neither you nor your kingship will endure to have." (1 Samuel 20:30 f.).

Saul cursed his son and called his friendship with David a shame. It's a clear indication that Saul knew Jonathan and David were not just friends. Sneeringly, he valued the friendship. Saul sensed the love between David and Jonathan and considered it dangerous. For it blew up all known norms and rules, which were aligned to power retention and order in the royal family. Saul became so angry that he even threw a spear at his own son. Then

Jonathan realized that the gap between Saul and David was no longer kitten. The abyss was unbridgeable. The competition between the two had turned Kamf into life and death. Jonathan could not communicate there. He had to decide now. He stayed outside with his father.

Jonathan and David met in secret and renewed their covenant. Jonathan asked David to spare his offspring and those of Saul. Perhaps Jonathan already guessed that he himself had no future at court. Then they took leave.

"David fell on his face to the earth and bowed down three times, and they kissed one another and wept together, but most of all David and Jonathan said to David, Go with peace, for what we both swore in the name of God, God stood between me and you, between my descendants and your descendants forever, and David got up and went his way, but Jonathan went into the city. " (1 Samuel 20, 41 ff.).

It was the last time they saw each other. It's a touching farewell scene. And she is told amazingly frankly. Both kissed and cried. And David the most. Here is also reported for the first time by David that he loved Jonathan. The two men had to say goodbye. Her love could not be and had no future. Two men crying. After the then male image that could not go well. They were men and soldiers. You should be brave and strong. Crying was not planned there. Certainly not a cry around each other. That was true at the time and still applies in many places today. The fact that the two also kissed and loved did not make things easier.

Although it has been proven by extra-biblical sources that men also had homoerotic love affairs at the time. That was quite common. At the same time, they had to be married and have children. Men should be real guys. Homoerotic sex did not contradict that. As long as they did not give themselves 'unmanly' and they did not break the usual male image. Only when they looked too feminine, too sensitive or seemingly too feminine, they were considered feminized or effeminate men. Then they had to fear sanctions and were excluded from the community. Because they endangered the existing gender order.

The story of David and Jonathan must have been remarkable at biblical times. Otherwise she would not have made it to the Bible in that open language and clarity. It is also noteworthy that their friendship in history was not condemned or moralized. Her love was just there and shaped the actions of young men. And at the same time, they were different again. David's biblically testifies that he had several wives. He was obviously a womanizer. But we do not read of such a deep love like Jonathan's at any other place in the Bible.

After the farewell between Jonathan and David, there was another battle against the Philistines. Saul and Jonathan did not survive the battle. His brothers did not survive either. When David heard about it, he began a lamentation:

"Israel, your pride is slain on your heights! Oh, the heroes have fallen!" Saul and Jonathan, the beloved and dear, in life and in death, they are not separated They were faster than eagles, were stronger than lions, you daughters of Israel You have to cry to Saul, he has dressed you in delicious purple, has put golden ornaments on your robes, too, the heroes have fallen in the midst of battle, Jonathan lies slain on the heights, woe is it for you, my brother Jonathan "I have had great joy and delight in you, you have been very dear to me." "More wonderful was your love for me than the love of women." Also, the handshakes have fallen, the weapons of battle lost. " (2 Samuel, 1, 1 ff.)

This lament makes it clear how strongly David Jonathan was inwardly attached. The lines remind me of Old Shatterhandwhen he died the death of his blood brother Winnetoucomplains, kisses him dying and is completely desperate. The homoerotic love is clearly felt. Nevertheless, she was not allowed to be named. She was dressed in deference and in praise of bravery and valor and encoded accordingly. Another language between men was not possible. Nevertheless, David was at the end of his lawsuit surprisingly clear:

"More wonderful was your love for me than the love of women."

More clearly, one should think that a declaration of love cannot be. Certainly not in a biblical book written down centuries before Christ's birth. And yet, this love was discussed away, relativized and sidelined. It was marked as friendship, at best as brotherly love. Because what could not be. The heteronormative standards allowed nothing else. The story should best be seen and forgotten as a side note in the life of the brave and prosperous Shepherd of David, who rose to be King of Israel. It was impossible for the most famous king of ancient Israel to love a man. Therefore it should not be told further.

Finally, the question remains. What was that relationship between the two men? My Answer: It was a relationship that touched me personally. It was a relationship in which the lovers became vulnerable and took risks. The relationship disturbed the logic of maintaining power, men's competition, fame and glory, and opposed it to something else: love, vulnerability and closeness. Attributes that are not and are not necessarily provided for men.

Was this friendship homoerotic? Has sexuality also played a role or not? Were the two men bisexual? We can not give answers to this from biblical history. That is not crucial. For beyond all heteronomous action patterns, history is above all a story of a touching friendship between men. It does without labels and categorization. Like the friendship between men in the movie " Brokeback MountainAnd yet one thing is clear: two men have loved each other, they have sworn allegiance and have not betrayed themselves to all power-minded people, they have become familiar, kissed and cried together.

If relationships are lived that way, then they deserve respect. No matter what they are called. Because love is diverse, overwhelming, and it can push boundaries. Human emotions are so much richer and more complex than prohibitions and norms. As long as they are lived in the mutual investment, in respect and respect of the human dignity of the opposite.

David and Jonathan have shown some of this wealth of human emotions. Good that people today can live such feelings. Even though it is still not easy or even life-threatening to show it in many places today.

WHY DAVID HAS TO FLEE

Why David has to flee

AFTER David Goliath has killed, Abner commander brings him to Saul. Saul is very happy. He makes David the leader of the army and lets him live in the palace.

Later, when the army returns from fighting the Philistines, the women sing, "Saul killed thousands, but David tens of thousands." Saul becomes jealous because David gets more honor. But Saul's son Jonathan is not jealous. He loves David very much and David likes Jonathan very much. The two promise that they will always be friends.

The angry King Saul

David is good at playing the harp and Saul likes to listen to him. But one day Saul does something terrible out of sheer jealousy. When David is playing the harp, Saul takes his spear and hurls it at David. He says, "I'll pin him on the wall!" But David jumps to the side and the spear flies past. The same happens to Saul again later. David now knows that he has to be very careful.

Do you still remember what Saul promised the man who killed Goliath? He wanted to give his daughter to him. But now he says that David would only get his daughter Michal if he kills a hundred Philistines. Imagine that! In reality, Saul hopes the Philistines will kill David. But they can not do that, so David marries Saul's daughter.

One day, Saul tells Jonathan and all his servants that he wants to kill David. But Jonathan says to his father, "Do not do anything to David! He did not hurt you either. He always helped you. When he fought Goliath, he could have even died. And you were glad he was so brave. "

90

Saul listens to his son and promises that he will do nothing to David. David returns to the palace. But when he plays the harp again, Saul throws his spear at him again. David dodges and the spear hits the wall. This is already the third time! David now knows that he has to flee.

In the evening David goes to his own house. But Saul sends a few men after him to kill him. Michal knows what her father is up to. She tells her husband, "If you do not flee tonight, you're dead tomorrow." Then she helps him escape through a window. For about seven years, David has to hide in different places so that Saul will not find him.

David in Exile

David in Nob

David fled south to the mountains of Judah, his home. He needed food and weapons. These he obtained from the city of Nob, which lies about half-way between Gibeah and Beth-Lehem. Nob was at that time a holy place, distinguished by the Sanctuary and priesthood. It became a holy city after the destruction of Shiloh. Weak, and almost fainting from his long flight, David appeared before the priest Ahimelech, who knew him well as the captain, friend, and son-in-law of Saul. He asked Ahimelech for some bread. He then asked for a sword; and as there was none in the place except that which he himself had taken from the giant Goliath, and which had been preserved ever since in the Sanctuary, David took possession of it, and hastily departed. But all that he had done in Nob had been carefully noticed by Doeg the Edomite, whose treachery was soon to be revealed.

David in Gath

David must indeed have been in great perplexity; for he saw no alternative but to flee to Gath, a chief town of his bitterest enemies, the Philistines, with the very sword of their slaughtered champion at his side. He hoped that he would not be recognized and that he might be permitted to stay in town as a hapless stranger. But his hope proved false; the servants of Achish, the king of Gath, said to their master, "Is not this David, the king of the land? Did they not sing one to another of him in dances, saying, 'Saul has slain his thousands and David his ten thousands'?" When David heard this, he was justly afraid. To save himself, he simulated madness, and thus he was allowed to leave the town in peace.

David in Adullam

David then escaped eastward, and sought refuge in one of the caves near Adullam, in the plain of Judah, between Beth-Lehem and Hebron. It was a secure retreat, where his brothers and all his father's house came to him. His solitary abode was soon known, and he was joined by many that were in distress, or in debt, or had any other cause of discontent.

They flocked to him, because they trusted his valor and wisdom, to save them from their troubles and to shield them against persecution. Thus four hundred men were gathered around him, over whom he had supreme command, like a great outlaw captain. He then proceeded to Mizpah, in the land of Moab, and entreated the king to afford shelter to his father and mother, as long as his own fate was so uncertain and full of danger. The heathen monarch consented. Then David, advised by the prophet Gad, who was faithfully attached to him, went with his followers to encamp in the forest of Hareth in Judah.

The Treacherous Doeg

Saul meanwhile was anxiously awaiting news about David, of whose movements he was entirely ignorant. One day he was sitting, spear in hand, beneath a tamarisk-tree at Gibeah, surrounded by his ministers and councillors, when Doeg the Edomite stepped forward, related all he had seen of David in Nob, and told him of Ahimelech's, the priest's, readiness in giving him bread and Goliath's sword. Saul's rage was kindled by this account; he sent at once for Ahimelech and all the priests of Nob. They came at his bidding and were fiercely upbraided for their conduct in favoring

David's flight. Ahimelech replied calmly and truthfully, "Who is so faithful among all thy servants as David, who is the king's son-in-law, and goes out at thy bidding, and is honored in the house?" But Saul, in his passion, ordered the instant death of the priests. No Jew could be found to commit so impious a crime. Doeg the Edomite alone consented to execute the horrible command. Ahimelech and all his guiltless priests, eighty-five in number, were slain on that day. One man alone escaped—Abiathar, the son of Ahimelech; he fled to David, was cordially received, and remained with the fugitive, sharing his perils and wanderings.

David Saves Keilah

David next undertook an expedition against the Philistines, who were pilfering the granaries of Keilah, a city in Judah.

He attacked the Philistines vigorously and drove them back with great slaughter. After David had thus rescued Keilah by a daring exploit, his own life was in danger from its ungrateful inhabitants. When Saul heard what David had done and that he was still within the walled city of Keilah, he considered it a good opportunity to surround the city and seize him, and resolved to march out against Keilah. But David, distrustful of the people, who would surely have delivered him up to the king, hastily departed, and fled with his six hundred followers to the desert land south of Hebron, where the Wilderness of Ziph and that of Maon afforded welcome retreats and hiding-places. When Saul heard that David had left Keilah, he desisted from the intended expedition.

David and Jonathan Meet Again

It was in the wilderness of Ziph that Jonathan had one last stealthy interview with David. He came full of affection and solicitude, and "strengthened David's courage in G‑d." "Fear not," he said, "for the hand of Saul my father shall not find thee, and thou shalt be king over Israel, and I will be next to thee, and that also Saul my father knows." In that lonely wilderness of Ziph, the outlaw and the king's son confirmed their old vows, and there they parted forever.

David in Ziph

While dwelling in the desert of Ziph, David nearly fell into the hands of Saul; for some persons, living in the neighboring districts, went up to Gibeah, and betrayed his retreat to the king. When David heard of Saul's approach he left Ziph, and sought safety in the more distant wilderness of Maon.

Saul pursued and discovered him and would surely have enclosed him and all his men, had not the sudden alarm of a Philistine invasion compelled Saul to a hasty return. But David proceeded to Engedi, eastward of Hebron, where he hoped to find a secure stronghold in the rocky cliffs on the shore of the Dead Sea. When Saul had returned from chastising the Philistines, he resumed his pursuit of David with fresh ardor. He took with him three thousand men, and with this host he scoured the mountains, searching for David from rock to rock and cave to cave.

David Spares Saul's Life

Once in this desperate chase, Saul fell into the hands of David. The wearied king had entered a cave to take some rest; and David, surrounded by his band, lay concealed in that very den. He held Saul now wholly in his power, and his followers would have made him believe that this chance was providentially sent to rid him of his foe, and to ensure his safety forever. But David shrank from the suggestion and, softly approaching Saul, he cut off the skirt of his robe. But he instantly repented even of this act, which might be construed as a want of the respect which he owed to the anointed of the L-rd. He waited quietly until Saul had left the cave; then following him and remaining at some distance, he greeted the king with the utmost respect and made himself known. It was a touching scene between the unhappy king and the object of his jealous hatred: David gentle and humble, Saul sorrow-laden and contrite, and now aware how far above him stood the son of Jesse. "Thou art more righteous than I," Saul said, "for thou hast requited me good, whereas I have requited thee evil." They parted in friendship, Saul returning to his residence in Gibeah, and David to his followers in the dreary cliffs.

Death of Samuel

About this time Samuel died at Ramah, his birthplace, where he had long lived in retirement. Yet, though apparently passing his closing years in isolation, he had still remained the guiding spirit of his time. He was deeply and sincerely lamented throughout the land. His remains were interred at Ramah, where the people assembled from far and near to pay the last honors to their great leader.

David and Nabal

David was still a vagabond king when he sought refuge in the desert of Maon. There lived in Carmel, not far distant, a very wealthy man of the name of Nabal, whose sheep and goats, as they grazed upon the surrounding pastures, had been protected by David and his men. Nabal was a churlish and evil-disposed miser, foolish and hardhearted; but his wife Abigail was as beautiful as she was charitable and intelligent. It was the time of the sheep-shearing, a season of great feasting and merry-making in the household of Nabal. So David sent ten of his followers to Carmel to ask for some present of provisions, in return for the services he had rendered to Nabal's shepherds. But the graceless Nabal insultingly refused the req uest.

David at once set out for the house of Nabal, in the company of four hundred of his followers. But one of Nabal's servants warned his mistress Abigail of the danger which threatened the whole household because of her husband's harshness and folly. As David was approaching Mount Carmel, he met a train of laden donkeys winding slowly towards him; they carried large q uantities of bread and meat and wine; dried corn, clusters of raisins, and cakes of figs; and last of all came Abigail. As soon as she perceived David, she alighted, and bowed herself humbly before him.

Abigail's wisdom and generosity surely saved Nabal and his household, and David was grateful to her for having prevented him from shedding blood. He accepted her presents and dismissed her thankfully. On the following morning, after a night spent by Nabal in feasting and drunkenness, Abigail told him of her meeting with David, and how she had barely averted the extermination of his entire household. Nabal was struck with consternation from which he never recovered; and ten days later he died. Not long afterwards, David asked Abigail to become his wife; she consented, and joined him in his mountain retreat.

David Spares Saul Again

Saul continued to pursue the exiled David, who was now concealed among the hills of Hachilah, in the east of the wilderness.

It was night, and the king's host had encamped in the valley below Hachilah, when David, who had carefully watched their movements, emerged from his hiding-place. Saul lay asleep in the trench, his spear fixed in the ground before him and a cruse of water by his side. His soldiers, led by Abner, were encamped near him. All had fallen asleep, and complete calmness prevailed. Once again the life of his great adversary was in David's hand. Followed by the brave and intrepid Abishai, the brother of Joab, he descended the hillside, and stood within the enemy's camp. Abishai was urging him to take revenge. But again David's feeling of reverence proved Saul's protection. "Destroy him not," he replied, "for who can stretch forth his hand against the L-rd's anointed, and be guiltless?" Yet he softly seized the spear and cruse of water, and carried them away.

David ascended the opposite hill, and from thence called out loudly to Abner. His voice came ringing down into the valley to the camp of Saul. He spoke stinging words of reproach to the captain of the host, who was keeping so negligent and faithless a watch by the side of his king. "As the L-rd lives," he concluded, "you are worthy to die, because you have not guarded your master, the L-rd's anointed; and now see where the king's spear is, and the cruse of water that was near his head!" Saul recognized the voice of David.

99

His conscience smote him; his bitter jealousy died away for the moment. He received his spear again and departed from David with these words: "Blessed be thou, my son David; thou shalt undertake great things, and shalt also prevail." The two men met no more.

David in Ziklag

Tired of constant wandering and flight, David determined to leave the territory of Judah and to proceed into the land of the Philistines, where his enemy was not likely to pursue him. So he went westward with his six hundred tried and chosen followers and presented himself before Achish, King of Gath. This monarch received him kindly, and not only allowed him to live in Gath, but also gave him and his men the town of Ziklag for a possession.

From Ziklag David carried on active warfare against the Amalekites. Achish heard confused rumors of these expeditions; but David led him to believe that his arms were turned against his own countrymen in the south of Judah, and that he was thus fighting for Achish no less than for himself. In this manner, the friendship of the Philistine chief towards David was steadily strengthened.

Death of King Saul

The Philistines Attack Again

Once again the Philistines under Achish resolved upon attacking the land of Israel. So complete was the trust of Achish in David, that he claimed the latter's help, and appointed him the chief of his bodyguard. The Philistine army marched out at once and pitched its camp at Shunem, in the very heart of the hostile country, in the district of Issachar, between the mountains of Tabor and Gilboa.

Saul and the Witch of Endor

The new Philistine invasion greatly alarmed Saul. Though his heart bode him ill, he quickly led forth his army and encamped at Gilboa. Anxiously, King Saul turned to G- d for help and counsel; but neither by dream, nor by vision, nor by prophets, did he obtain the wished-for advice. Goaded to despair, he bethought himself at last of the witches who were believed to be able to raise the dead and to cause them to communicate with the living. To a woman of Endor, Saul determined to resort for help. Disguising himself, he went to her house at nightfall with two companions.

At first the woman was afraid, for witchcraft was forbidden in Israel on penalty of death. Saul, however, swore that nothing should happen to her and

101

bade her call up the spirit of Samuel. The woman obeyed and proceeded to practice her strange art.

Presently the spirit of Samuel appeared and informed Saul that the battle with the Philistines would be lost and that Saul and his sons would die. Saul fell prostrate to the ground, fainting. For a long time he refused to rise and to refresh himself; at last the entreaties of his companions and the woman prevailed upon him to sit down to the meal she had prepared, for he had tasted no food all the preceding day and night.

David Returns to Ziklag

Meanwhile, all the chiefs of the Philistines had united their forces into one vast army. David and his six hundred followers were in the rear of Achish. When the Philistine leaders saw them, they would not allow David, their most dangerous enemy, who had humbled them repeatedly, to remain in their midst during the battle, and they pressed upon Achish to dismiss him and his band.

David had to return to Ziklag with his followers. But mournful and desolate was the sight which met him upon his return. The Amalekites, taking advantage of the defenseless state of the country, had among other deeds of violence, sacked and burnt Ziklag, led away its flocks and herds, its women and children, and seized their property. David's own two wives were among the captives. A loud wail of horror and despair burst from the bereaved Israelites who, in their anger, threatened the life of David, to whom they imputed their misfortunes. But David soothed the rage of his men, and at once announced his intention of pursuing the audacious invaders. He led his soldiers in breathless haste southward; but only four hundred of them could endure this exhausting march, the rest remained behind, wearied and fainting before they crossed the brook Bezor. On his march, David found an Egyptian in the fields, apparently dead. He carefully tended and refreshed him, and thus saved his life. Asked who he was, this man related that he had been ill and had, therefore, been left behind by his Amalekite master when the army returned from burning Ziklag, and that he had lain in the fields for three days and three nights without food. The Egyptian, on receiving the solemn pledge that he would not be delivered up to his former master, was ready to lead David and his soldiers to the camp of the enemy.

The Amalekites were feasting and reveling in the camp, surrounded by their recently acq uired spoil, when they were surprised by David and his handful of followers and completely routed. Four hundred young men alone of the vast host of the heathen escaped upon their swift camels. All the captive women and children of the Israelites were rescued; not one of them was missing; all their property was recovered, and, in addition to it, immense booty was taken from the invaders. The conquerors returned joyful and happy to their brethren at Bezor, with whom they divided the spoil.

Death of Saul and Jonathan

While David was fighting the Amalekites, a furious battle was raging between the Philistines and the Jews.

The tide of battle swiftly turned against the Jews, as Samuel had predicted, and Saul's army was utterly routed. The king's own sons Jonathan, Abinadab, and Malkishua were among the slain. Many fled for their lives. Saul was severely wounded by the Philistine archers. Then, giving up all hope and dreading the thought of falling into the hands of his heathen enemies, he called upon his armor-bearer to slay him. But the man was afraid and durst not obey. Saul, therefore, fell upon his sword to kill himself. However, the wound not proving immediately mortal, he entreated an Amalekite who had by chance come near the place, to pierce him with his sword, and the stranger, seeing that the king could not possibly recover, did as he was requested. Saul's armor-bearer, now unwilling to live, died also by his own hand. The Philistines then occupied without a struggle many of the Hebrew towns, deserted by their inhabitants who had fled in despair. On the next day, the Philistines came to the battle-field to strip the slain. When they recognized the bodies of the king and of his three sons, they set up a wild shout of rejoicing, cut off Saul's head, and took his arms, which they sent to their own country to be kept in a chief temple of Ashtarte; but the bodies of Saul and of his sons they fixed on the wall of Beth-Shan, a town not far from the Jordan opposite to the territory of Gilead. They were rescued, however, by the brave men of Jabesh, who brought them into their town and buried them under a tamarisk-tree. All the people kept a fast for seven days.

David Mourns for Saul and Jonathan

David was in Ziklag, confident that the great heroes of Israel, Saul and Jonathan, would once again, with G-d's help, prevail over the enemy. But soon he was stunned with grief. There came running into the city a messenger with his blood-stained clothes rent, and with earth upon his head. He bore in his hand the royal crown and bracelet, which he laid before David with all signs of homage. He then related the defeat of the Israelites and the death of Saul and his sons. Grief and mourning prevailed among the Jews of Ziklag. All tore their garments and abstained from food that day.

David sincerely mourned the death of Saul and Jonathan and the defeat of Israel. In a lament he composed over the fallen princes, David proved his deep affection for Saul and Jonathan, and his sincere grief at the terrible catastrophe that had befallen Israel

GARY FORTY

Made in the USA
Monee, IL
22 February 2022

91656089R00066